Big Things

Written by Jo Windsor

Rigby

Here is a big plane.
The big plane can go up
in the sky.

plane

Look at this big helicopter.
This helicopter can go up
in the sky, too.

helicopter

Here is a big train.
The big train has
big wheels.

big wheel

6

train

truck

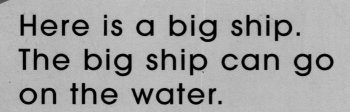

Here is a big ship.
The big ship can go
on the water.

MAERSK SEALAND

ship

Look at this!
This is a big, big ship.
The planes can go on
the big ship.

ship

Index

big helicopter...................4

big plane...................2

big ship...................10, 12

big train...................6

big truck...................8

Guide Notes

Title: Big Things
Stage: Early (1) – Red

Genre: Nonfiction (Expository)
Approach: Guided Reading
Processes: Thinking Critically, Exploring Language, Processing Information
Written and Visual Focus: Photographs (static images), Index, Labels
Word Count: 81

THINKING CRITICALLY

(sample questions)
- Tell the children that this book is about things that are big.
- Look at the title and read it to the children.
- Ask the children what they know about different things that are very big.
- Focus the children's attention on the Index. Ask: "What are you going to find out about in this book?"
- If you want to find out about a big plane, on which page would you look?
- If you want to find out about a big truck, on which page would you look?
- Why do you think planes would land on the big, big ship?
- Look at page 8. How do you know that wheel is very big?

EXPLORING LANGUAGE

Terminology
Title, cover, photographs, author, photographers

Vocabulary
Interest words: plane, helicopter, train, wheels, ship, truck
High-frequency words (reinforced): up, too
Positional words: up, in, on

Print Conventions
Capital letter for sentence beginnings, periods, commas, exclamation mark